Jess and Trevor Go on a Trip

by Dana Catharine
illustrated by Toni Goffe

Printed in the United States of America

ISBN 0-15-317259-2 – Jesse and Trevor Go on a Trip

Ordering Options
ISBN 0-15-318631-3 (Package of 5)
ISBN 0-15-316986-9 (Grade 2 Package)

1 2 3 4 5 6 7 8 9 10 179 02 01 00 99

Jesse and Trevor are good friends.
Trevor is going with Jesse to visit Jesse's
relatives in the city. "I always have fun in
the city," says Jesse. "My relatives said they
will take us to skate at the ice palace!"

1

"I packed my own luggage for the trip,"
Trevor tells Jesse. "It's a good thing our
luggage is not the same. We can tell it
apart by the color."

2

Jesse and Trevor take their luggage to
the car. Oh, no! They both drop their
luggage!

It's a good thing the luggage is
so sturdy!

Everyone gets into the car and buckles up a seat belt. Then Jesse's Dad begins the drive. It's a good thing that Jesse and Trevor are such good companions. It will be a very long drive!

4

"Can we listen to a cassette?" asks Trevor. "I want to hear some music."

"I want to listen to a story cassette," says Jesse. "I don't want music!"

"Are you boys being good companions now?" asks Jesse's mom.

The boys have to make a choice. Will
they listen to music? Will they listen to
a story?

"I know," says Jesse. "We can listen to
music for a little while. Then we can listen
to a story."

The boys are good companions again!

While the boys are listening to the
cassettes, they have a snack. Jesse eats an
orange. Trevor eats apple slices and a piece
of cheese.

"Let's play a game," says Jesse's mom. "We will count cars for the next five miles."

Jesse counts red cars, Trevor counts blue cars, and Jesse's mom counts trucks. Who counts the most?

"I want to play a different game," says Jesse. "I will ask a riddle. You figure out the answer. Here is my riddle. *We are very small. We are gray. We squeak. What are we?*"

"Mice!" says Trevor. "You are mice!
Now it's my turn."

"Here is my riddle," says Trevor. "*You can go places on me. I have two wheels. I have a horn or a bell, too! What am I?*"

"I know that," says Jesse. "You are a
bicycle, just like my own sturdy bicycle!"

"Look, boys, we're in the city!" said
Jesse's dad. "You were having so much fun,
you didn't notice that we arrived!"

Travel Time

Jesse and Trevor played a game and asked riddles on their long car trip. Think of something else that would be fun to do in a car. On a sheet of paper, write a few sentences telling about this game or activity. Share your idea with classmates.

School-Home Connection Ask your child to read *Jesse and Trevor Go on a Trip* to you. Then ask your child to tell about the travel time idea he or she wrote about.

TAKE-HOME BOOK
Just in Time
Use with "Dinosaurs Travel."